T0197341

Protection

How far would you go to save a brother?

Aliza Yazdani

Order this book online at www.trafford.com
or email orders@trafford.com

Most Trafford titles are also available at major online book retailers.

Printed in the United States of America.

ISBN: 978-1-4669-0895-6 (sc)
ISBN: 978-1-4669-0896-3 (e)

Trafford rev. 1/25/2012

 www.trafford.com

North America & international
toll-free: 1 888 232 4444 (USA & Canada)
phone: 250 383 6864 ♦ fax: 812 355 4082

For anyone who thinks they're the only one
Still playing pretend.

The games of four friends and neighbors inspired this book: Aliza Yazdani, Zach Yazdani, Will Christensen, and Theresa Christensen.

Illustration on page iii by Elizabeth Meyers.

Editing by Theresa Christensen

CHARACTERS

Jessica Clease — age: 9, Power: Electricity, citizen of the USA.

Grace Clease — age: 11, Power: Water, citizen of the USA.

Grant Clease — age: 10, Power: Darkness, citizen of the USA.

Jake Clease — age: 6, Power: none, citizen of the USA.

Samantha Reaner — age: 9, Power: Electricity, citizen of the USA.

Peter Johnson — age: 11, Power: Electricity, citizen of the USA.

Jose Fellin — age: 9, Power: Electricity, citizen of Mexico.

John Jap — age: 9, Power: Electricity, citizen of Jupiter.

Daniella Heaven — age: 9, Power: Water, citizen of Israel.

Hannah Bashca — age: 11, Power: Water, citizen of England.

Esmerelda Bentch — age: 11, Power: Electricity, citizen of Hungary.

James Johnson — age: 9, Power: Fire, citizen of the USA.

Robert Johnson — age: 9, Power: Light, citizen of the USA.

Scarlett Leonard — age: 10, Power: Darkness, citizen of Italy.

Sean de Hierro — age: 12, Power: Metal, citizen of Colombia.

GLOSSARY

Form: People who get the same Power at the same time and are the same age. For example, Jess' form her first year is E9-1.

Goes: an elevator-like transportation that rockets from one building to another within a planet.

JAP: Jupiter Academy for Powers, the school for training kids with a Power.

Master: a Power teacher who teaches one form until that form graduates. For example Rick is Jess's Master.

Power: a supernatural ability, including Electricity, Darkness, Water.

CHAPTER 1

"Do not protect yourself by a fence, but rather by your friends"

—*Czech Proverb*

It was noon on a hot August day, and two of my three siblings and I sat in our small orphanage bedroom, in New York City.

"Jess, plug in the fan," ordered Grace, my eleven year old sister. She struggled to turn around in the recliner and pushed me out of the space next to her.

I began to object, but my sister's ocean-blue-eyes practically shot lasers at me. Sighing, I stood and relinquished the overstuffed chair to her.

"Thanks," muttered Grace, settling back into her mane of flowing blue hair, but she wasn't able to relax for long. Her face was suddenly confronted with our brother's rear end. He enjoyed the comfortable chair almost as much as Grace did.

"Grant! Ugh! Not Funny!" With an enormous heave and not a small amount of water coming out of Grace's hand, Grant (my ten year old brother who had scrambled on top of Grace) was launched across the room.

"Graaa-aaace! Why'd you do that!?" His black eyes flashing, he shook out his shaggy jet-black hair, and once he was relatively dry, sent a good-sized ball of Darkness (his Power) at the wall above our exuberant sister's head.

For good reason, Grant hadn't risked a full out fight with our older and more powerful sister. An entire year of training at JAP (I didn't know what this stood for, but

I hoped to soon find out) was not something to be trifled with, as Grant well knew. After every summer since they had gotten their Powers, the two of them left for a day's trip via bus, after which they traveled to the school. I'd never been there, because I had yet to discover my power, but with any luck, this fall the Clease dorm room at JAP would be the home to one more pupil.

Of course, both of my parents had had powers, and the gene was passed on to all of us. At least, that's what I hoped for. At nine, I was a little late in discovering my power. There was still hope, though. Grant and Grace had also gotten their powers at my age.

I remembered all this as I set off on the rather dangerous trek across the room. Water and I had never been the best of friends. Of course, that fact wouldn't keep Grace from forcing me to plug in the fan. Electricity was too bright for Grant because he, like the myths of vampires, hated light. And Grace, having water running to every possible part of her body, didn't fair much better. So I picked up the plug, and went to the outlet. As the plug went into the outlet, a huge spark came out and hit me in the head.

"Jess! Are you okay?" Grace came running.

"Yeah I . . . I think so" I said shakily.

"No burn, no scratch, no nothing?" Grace asked, puzzled.

"Uh-uh" I said. I touched my forehead. It wasn't even tender. Hmmm.

"You didn't feel it?"

"No, but I saw it." Now I was a little bit worried. What did it mean that a literal bolt of lightning had entered my head and I had not felt even the slightest thing?

Grant and Grace had a quick discussion in hushed tones. There were a lot of glances back over their shoulders in my direction and shaking of heads. Finally, they turned around, worried looks on their faces.

"Jess", Grace said with an edge to her voice. "I think you have Electricity".

"That's great," I cried. "Why are you so upset? I get to come with you to JAP and study and everyth . . ." My voice trailed off. Grace was shaking her head. She looked like she was on the verge of tears.

"Don't you get it?" she cried. "I have Water! The opposite, we have each other's strongest weaknesses."

Oh. That would explain a lot. Ugh. *This* would complicate things during our fights.

CHAPTER 2

I lay awake in bed, trying to blur out yesterday's memory. I was trying desperately to convince myself that yesterday was a dream. It had to be, but then again, it just *couldn't* be.

At breakfast, Grace and Grant acted as if nothing were different. I soon saw why. Jake, my younger brother, was in the room. Being only six, he still hadn't gotten over the I-want-what-you-have stage, and would likely throw a fit when he found out I had my power.

"Am I going?" I asked my older siblings. I was choosing my words with care to keep the impending tantrum at bay.

"Going where? Can superhero me go? Superhero, that's me." Jake sing-songed. He was into those kiddy shows and superheroes.

"You're not a superhero, Jakey, but that doesn't matter," Grant chuckled. "Jess, you're going to school with us right after breakfast."

I was too surprised to speak.

"No, not school!" wailed Jake slopping his cereal on the table, "I don't want to be alone!"

Grace gave him a hug, while cleaning up his mess.

"Jess, go and get your most prized possession. You won't need anything else," ordered Grant, though his tone was almost proud, which was weird, because Grant liked to act like didn't care about me or anything else.

I ran up the metal stairs in the orphanage. I had to go up three stories before reaching the hall to my room. On the way I did some thinking. I had a power, Electricity. I was going to JAP. Soon I would be learning how to fight like my older siblings.

I burst into my room, started digging around, finding things like old CDs and trophies from gym. I had gotten them for running the mile faster than anyone in my class. I had always been fast for my age. Now I realized that it was because I had Electricity, but it had been too undeveloped to be noticed.

This was the last time I would be in here until next summer. Or so I thought.

CHAPTER 3

Coming back into the orphanage dining area with a picture of my siblings and me, updated every year, I saw that Grace and Grant were waiting.

"Okay, now we wait outside for the bus," said Grace.

"How does it know we're waiting?" I asked.

"You," Grant said simply, a "man" of few words.

I had to guess. Probably when I got my Power, it alerted someone either on the bus or at the school.

It took ten minutes for the silver bus to arrive. When it did, it stopped and opened its doors. I guessed it was about half the size of a football field. The weirdest part though was that even though we were out in the open, tourists and workers and everyone who were walking past didn't see it at all!

Once inside I noticed that the first ten rows were like normal bus seats, but the next ten were grubby and full of plant life. The next five rows back had a bubble of water around the seats. The next twenty-five rows had other elements engulfing five rows each. The aisle was clear of these elements. But I could not see the back of the bus because even the aisle was covered with Darkness.

One guy in what I assumed was the Fire section looked right at me and winked. He wore a shirt for the Fantastic Four that said 'Flame on!' He looked about my age, new to the bus as well by the way he kept looking around, and pretty cocky judging by that wink he gave me. I gave him my best *I don't think so* smile, squinting my eyes and cocking my head, making him snicker, and went back to inspecting the sections.

CHAPTER 4

As I looked around, Grace spoke to a lean teenage boy. He wore a clean white jump suit with short sleeves. Over the left side of his chest was a badge with writing on it. It said: Ned L.: N17-15.

Grant spoke to me, "I'm going to sit down, I don't like all this light and we have a day's ride ahead of us so get settled. Just call Ned if you need anything, he's really nice. Plus he's been here for 15 years, since he was 2."

Before I could answer, he disappeared into the dark area in the back of the bus. Then Grace slid through the bubble of water as though it were the most normal thing in the world.

"All right, Jessica Clease! E9-1. I'll get you a seat with other girls in your form," rattled Ned.

"What's a form?" I asked now curious, but feeling a bit dumb.

Ned grinned as he led me down the aisle. I noticed that about 10 kids were already sitting on the bus. Grace was sitting with two other girls her age, maybe in her form. They were making the water in the bubble they were sitting in spin around them.

"E9-1 is a form. That's a group of kids who have the same Power, the same age and came the same time as you." Ned interrupted my thoughts. "'E' stands for Electricity, 9 is your age, and 1 tells others that this is your first year here."

"Okay, so I just find someone in my form," I gulped. Being new is never fun and being new in a school for kids with powers and who (as I'm told) learn martial arts is even worse.

"I'll help you," said an older boy, sitting in the front of the Electricity section.

"Thanks, Nick" Ned said, relieved that he didn't need to help me.

"No prob, bro." Nick replied. I glanced at the two of them. Were they really brothers or was Nick just being all cool?

Nick walked ten steps down the aisle to the last row. There sat another girl my age with the same blond hair and hazel eyes.

"Jessica, Samantha. Samantha, Jessica. Bye!" Nick went back to his seat.

I sat down next to her. We both sat awkwardly, not knowing what to say. Then . . .

"Call me Jess." I said.

"OK." She said quietly.

Then Samantha and I started to chat, as the bus moved along, picking up other kids.

J   J   J   J   J

At about noon Ned passed out everyone's favorite food for lunch. I got a salad and a cheese pizza. By now Samantha and I were laughing and making jokes about the power of Plant, like old friends. Though I noticed she never disagreed with me, just went with everything I said.

Suddenly Ned stood up and yelled, "We're taking off, please keep your seatbelts on TIGHT."

"What does he mean by taking off?" I asked the boy across the aisle. He was what Grace would call "cute", blond hair and sparkling green eyes.

"Exactly what it sounds like, I guess." He shrugged.

"Hey, Jess," Samantha turned to me. "You said your last name was Clease, right?"

"Yeah, why?"

"Well, my dad told me that nine years ago a young couple drowned in a lake, but the bodies were never found. But the same year a boy and girl a year apart showed up at a orphanage, then a couple months later another girl. Three years later a fourth kid, a boy, landed in the same orphanage." Samantha started to get excited.

"So what does this have to do with my last name?"

"The couple and the kids all had the same last name, Clease. It's like the couple died, but they didn't,"

"What?! That makes no sense."

"I know, but the same thing happened with my older brother. All the newspapers said that he died when he fell of a roof, but I was there so I know he didn't, he got back up and laughed, and he still comes around to visit!"

"Okay that's weird," I was *so* confused.

"I know . . . Jess, I don't think your parents are dead." Samantha had a shine to her eyes.

"Neither do I," the boy across the aisle interjected, "This school tells the world that you are dead so you can work for them, as a master or mentor. And you get to choose how you *die*. But that only happens if you become an apprentice."

"When would that be?" I was so exited that I couldn't think straight.

"When you are 19."

"Peter," he said, holding out his hand.

"Jessica. And this is Samantha." I said shaking it.

J   J   J   J   J

"Hey, Peter you've been to this school before, right?" I looked out the window at the city I had called home for so long.

"Yeah, going on three years now. Why?"

"Well then what does J.A.P. stand for?"

"Jupiter Academy for Powers," He said knowingly.

"Is it on Jupiter?" I started to joke.

"Yeah it is", Peter grinned at our surprised faces, and "Yeah and our sort of rival, sort of enemy, is SAPT, Saturn Academy for Power Training. It's all just so people without powers don't ever find us."

"Whoa! So do we live on Jupiter? How long do we go to school? Then what happens after?" Thinking about this I realized my siblings never told me anything at all about the school I was about to attend. I was already learning so much and we hadn't even gotten to JAP yet!

"You can graduate from apprentice any time from 20 years old to 30 years old. It depends on how fast you learn and who your mentor is. But not everyone becomes an apprentice, it's only if you need more training." Peter seemed to enjoy our questions.

"My dad told me that there is a difference, at JAP, between a master and a mentor, but he didn't tell me what it was." Samantha got a question in.

"Oh yeah, there is. A master is a teacher at school for each power. There are normally at least two masters for each power. But if the Power is a more common one there can be more. Like for our power, Electricity, there is a master for every form. I have Patrick as a master; you'll probably have Rick, his younger brother. He had a form that graduated last year. Once you are 19 you are apprenticed to a mentor." He explained.

Was he always a walking encyclopedia? Facts, facts, facts. No options at all. If I were talking to him on the phone I would've hung up. "Oh, that's cool," I said. Then two other questions popped into my head, "How many kids are in one form? Can you learn anything other than how to use your power at school?"

"Yeah you can learn anything you want, but you always have to learn the required subjects like Math and stuff. By the way, Jessica," His face got red. "You're Grace Clease's sister, right?

"Yeah. Why?" I thought the look on his face was funny.

"Could you-. She-. I like her." Wow, why is he telling *me* this. I mean, that's just awkward.

After that Peter stopped acting like an encyclopedia, which was good, but he actually stopped talking to us altogether. So, Samantha and I went back to making fun of Plant. Why you ask? Well, because Plant is one of the weakest of the powers. Yes I know that it can kill a regular human by wrapping vines around the neck, but am I a regular human? No, I am not.

CHAPTER 5

After a long nap I woke up stiff and disoriented. The bus seemed strangely dark. Everything inside looked the same. Then I looked out the window. We were in space and I don't mean space, like air. I mean space like the great beyond, the final frontier. All I could see outside were stars and a bit of a planet, Grace later said was Mars. It looked like we were flying over it. When I asked Sam, she told me that we had been in space for the past hour. Wow, we were moving fast. Soon we would pass it.

Fifteen minutes later the bus, or I should say spaceship, dropped steeply and suddenly. All of us first years screamed, but all the other kids stayed calm. I guessed they were used to it.

Finally we leveled out and landed softly on a long docking bay. We had arrived.

"No one get up till the docking bay retracts completely", Ned yelled from the front, "then you will get out of the bus. First years will split into powers and wait to be given a tour. Everyone else may go to the cafeteria, library, training room, or dorm."

There was a lot of bustling to get off the bus. As we got into groups, I noticed that another bus was pulling up, and on the side was a big fat 'M'. I later would find out that it stood for Mexico. One boy came to our group. He had black hair with wisps of blond in it.

He spoke broken English, "Hola, ees thees el form E9-1?"

"Yeah, I mean, si," I sputtered.

"I am in your form, me llama Jose Fellin" He said

Just then another boy about my age stepped out of a door on the far wall. He looked quite at home. Why would he be here?

"Hi, I'm John, John Jap," he said as he walked toward us.

"Wait, Jap?" I said, surprised.

"Yeah, my granddad is the Headmaster." He said in a bored tone. I did notice that he said nothing about parents.

"So does that like give you special privileges, or something?" asked a girl who had walked down from the bus on the far end of the hanger. She looked nice but had blue highlights in her hair. I took a step back pulling Samantha with me.

"What?" She said

"Water," I said simply.

"Yeah, so? Oh all you have Electricity, oh well. I'm Daniella Heaven." We all shook hands with her. Then she walked down to the Water kids. Nick came over and took us over to the door on the far wall. He told John to go ahead to his dorm because he already knew his way around.

We followed Nick to the wall of the courtyard, it seemed to be covered in doors.

"Okay group, these are Goes. They're for transportation, like a one-man subway. Every room on Jupiter has it's own code, and you type it into this keypad here," He pointed to what looked like a futuristic calculator. "There is one pretty much everywhere all over the planet, including one for every dorm building, and they float around at close to light speed and land you in the location of your choice.

When I looked at the button pad, I saw that there were two parts to the panel; a part for the alphabet and a part for the numbers zero through nine. In the middle were two buttons. One said 'Enter' and the other had a dash on it.

"Cool! Like an elevator on steroids!" someone shouted from the back. Nick smiled and chuckled at the ignorance of the newcomers.

"Now I want you all to type in C-328 on a panel, then press enter, and when it opens, get in. One at a time into one of the Goes around the room." he instructed us.

"Get in! Then we'll be separated from the group," yelped a seven-year-old standing behind me.

"Yeah that's the point. Goes are one person transports." Nick said with decreasing patience. "Get *in.*"

Inside the Goes was cramped. All there was was a carpet, light panel and metal doors on every side. Being inside made me a bit sick with excitement about where I was and going to. I mean after such a long time of waiting I was finally at JAP, I had my power, and I was getting a tour of my new school.

When the Goes finally stopped, I stepped out into a cafeteria. It was huge, I bet a thousands kids could have eaten in here and there would still be room. Slowly, more and more of us appeared, and we huddled in a corner instinctively against the hubbub of hundreds of older kids laughing and bustling all around us. Finally, Nick appeared and we let out a collective sigh of relief.

Nick said you could go up to the front and asked for whatever you wanted. We got to try it for dinner. "All it takes is five seconds if anyone wants anything to eat," Nick called out. He led us up to the front and asked for a triple-decker ham and sardine sandwich with caviar and a glass of seltzer on the side.

"Yeah, I know it's gross. I'm not actually going to eat it. I'll give 30 bucks to anyone who does, so come talk to me after. But I was just trying to show that you really could get *anything* here. So, enjoy your dinner." He chuckled and walked to a table to sit and wait for anyone brave or stupid to take him up on his wager. Slowly, we all ordered our respective dinners and went to find seats.

J   J   J   J   J

After dinner we got to see the library, the nurse, and the office where adults tracked kids that could have a power. On the list of kids in the US, I saw Jake's name with a gold star next to it, but I didn't know what it meant . . . yet.

After that we went to the apprenticing and dueling rooms, which were just big round stadiums. I couldn't see what was so special about them . . . Though a lot of older kids who had tagged along for the tour started whispering and exchanging tense glances with each other as soon as got near them.

Then it was time to see the Electricity training room. Almost everything was made of rubber. I felt weak being enclosed in rubber. So did everyone else from the look of things. I assumed this was supposed to make us get stronger at fighting in rubber so that in a real fight we'd be ready.

It was getting late so Nick gave us each a slip of paper with a Goes code. Mine said C-125.

In a daze I stepped into the Goes. As the Goes took off I could now feel it swerving all over the place, up down and all around. When I stepped out I was in a domed room at the end of a long hallway. On the ceiling was a big 'C'. I was in a dorm building.

There it was, the dorm room I would be sharing with my siblings for the next ten years. Inside I found Grant sitting on a couch playing video games on a big flat screen TV.

"Grace is in her room, go check out yours." Grant suggested without taking his eyes off the screen.

"I will, later. I want to look around this one."

"Okay, suit yourself. I want to play this till lights out . . . Die, Nazis die!"

I looked around the room. You may ask, what did I see? Did I like it? What's not to like? A flat screen TV, a radio of the newest model, of course, a few couches, and what really blew my mind was a label under a picture that said 'Sally and Andrew Clease'. My parents, back when they were in their, oh, say twenties. My dad looked a lot like Grant and me, while my mom looked like Grace and Jake.

I guess Grant had been watching my slow tour because I heard his voice though the giant explosion that was going through my head. MY PARENTS! HERE! I guess I always knew they came here but seeing proof in the actual place was mind-boggling!

"Yeah. That's them, but we don't get to meet them till Jake has at least a year of training and that could be in nine years, or it could be never." Grant said all of a sudden.

"Where did you get nine and never?" I said, worried. Never meet my PARENTS!? If they're alive, I had to meet them.

"You need at least five years of training to be an apprentice otherwise you either have a really small power or you're a dud. Which is someone who had at least one parent who had a power but they don't, which Jake may just be. It's amazing our parents might have passed powers onto all four of us." Grant finished.

"Don't. Ever. Say. That." Grace literally steamed, making Grant and me step back. In her hands were large balls of water. I backed up towards my new room. I'd seen this fight a thousand times over the summer, and it was never pretty. Grant would come up with equal balls of darkness, then they would blow stuff up and someone always ended up on the floor unconscious. With that lovely thought in my head, I inched towards the door with my name on it.

"It's possible Jake could be a dud", Grant repeated, even though he knew it would start that kind of fight.

"No it is not. Jake has a power. Did you even see that star by his name? He *so* has a power." Grace yelled, spraying Grant with, you guessed it, water.

At that moment I decided to step into my new room, slamming the huge protective metal door behind me. I could already hear the sound of who knows what smashing and breaking.

A queen sized bed, a small nightstand, a closet full of jumpsuits that were mostly short sleeved except for one long sleeved, a desk with a chair, and a small bookshelf greeted me as I turned around. I even had my own bathroom!

It was *really* nice, but a little too much like a hotel for my taste. Too impersonal. I would need to do some trashing and rearranging to make it feel like home.

On the wall was a framed schedule that included times, Goes codes, and activities.

Wake up	7am	-
Breakfast	7:30am	C-328
Power class	8am	E-317
History of Powers Class	9am	P-726
Math Class	10am	M-284
English Class	10:30am	E-523
Power Class	11am	E-317
Lunch	12pm	C-328
Break	1pm	-
Gym	1:30pm	G-786
Karate	2pm	K-662
Break	3pm	-
Dinner	4pm	C-328
Lights out	10:30pm	-

So this was how my life would be for the next ten years on weekdays. That's a pretty good way to live. Could use a bit of variety, but I guessed I'd try and get that during classes.

I checked my watch. 10:25 pm, five minutes till lights out. Outside I heard my siblings' fight die down as they went to bed. Bed sounded good to me. I was soooooo tired.

As I was falling asleep I realized something mildly disturbing but mostly just annoying. You know . . . I never found out if John Jap did get special privileges or not.

CHAPTER 6

At seven in the morning my loud alarm clock woke me up. My first full day at JAP was about to start, and I wanted to be ready on time.

After getting dressed in a blue short-sleeved jumper, I went to wake up my siblings. When I looked I found Grant sitting on the couch again playing video games. So I went to wake up Grace. At her threshold I called her name. "Grace?"

Suddenly I was slammed against the opposite wall, soaking wet, stunned

"Grace!" I screamed in pain. Not only did my back hurt from being slammed against the wall, but also my body burned! Grace had hit me with the one thing that hurt the most, water. The worst part was that I hadn't done anything.

"Oh my god, oh my god! I'm so sorry Jess!" Grace shrieked, running over.

"Get that water off me!" I cried, tears running down my cheeks. Running her hand over the water on me, my big sister removed it from me. Then she helped me up and hugged me.

"Come on sweetheart, let's go to breakfast early, I'll introduce you to some of my friends. Grant, you coming?"

"Nah, I'm good. I'll meet you later." Grant replied, eyes fixated on the TV.

J   J   J   J   J

As Grace and I sat down at a table in the cafeteria, a shout rang out, "Loony!"

We looked up to see a short girl with blue-green hair bounding towards us.

"Hey crazy." Grace grinned and turned to me, "Jess, this is Hannah, she's insane. Be scared."

"Hey, hey, hey!" Another girl, this time blond, sing-sanged as she leapt over the table.

She hugged Grace and Hannah. "Okay, now, where's my boyfriend?"

"Ezzy!!" Grace drew out the nickname, exasperated.

"D*mn it girl, the year hasn't even started." Just then I realized that Hannah was English. I hadn't heard her accent very clearly before. "Well little loony, you have now met our resident manimizer, Esmeralda Bentch. It's like magic how those blokes just fall in love with her" Hannah said jokingly to me.

Grace didn't seem to get it as a joke. "That's not nice Hannah, Ezzy's just got a special charm."

"What's not nice?" It was Peter. I noticed that Grace blushed when she saw him. Maybe Peter's feelings for my sister were returned.

"Nothing." Esmeralda said, dismissing the matter.

"Hmm, okay. Anyway, Jess these are my twerp little brothers, James and Robert. You guys are all in 9-1."

Peter's younger brothers were twins by the look of them. Though one was a redhead and the other was blond, they looked a lot like Peter, but ten times more like each other.

"Hey, I remember you." The redhead said. It was the guy who winked at me, "you thought I was hot."

"James, I bet she was just being nice." The blond, who had to be Robert, said, "Honestly, if you were any more full of it, I would never had believed Peter when he said the when you get your Power, you start to mature faster. With you, no one can tell."

"When we get our Powers we start maturing faster?" This was news to me.

"Yeah or at least so says my brother says." James said.

"I've never noticed that." I said amazed.

"But only in certain ways. Don't ask, it might be Peter just talking. He does that sometimes. But yeah I think so, we grow up faster." Robert said. "It only kicks in when you've got your Power. It's like you're maturing with normal kids your age until that point, and then it speeds up. By maybe eighteen most of us are at the maturity level of most adults. Then it slows again when you're an adult, so you don't like die at like 40 or anything. You die when you would if you didn't have a Power" Robert explained. "it could just be Peter being the dork he normally is, but I kinda believe him."

Grant walked by and ruffled my hair. He was with a tall black guy, and a slender dark haired girl.

"'Sup little sis', this is Tommy and this is Scarlett. They're freaks, especially Scarlett."

"Thanks Grant." Scarlett said, dryly.

"Well I am a freak, I mean look at my eyes." Tommy's Chinese accent surprised me almost as much as his neon green eyes.

Breakfast was awesome. I had cereal and five pancakes. There were a lot of different things going on at once. Ezmerelda and her boyfriend were tickling each other, splashing milk all over the place. John and Jose were having a heated discussion in Spanish; don't ask me how John could speak Spanish, but he could, with a perfect accent and everything. Scarlett and Grant had been sitting at one end of the table, but when Robert and James sat down near by, they moved to the other end to get away. Dani and

Samantha were talking about how they got their powers, but I wanted to watch Hannah and Grace as they made some boy's water rise and fall. He was looking around to find out who was doing it but he never looked their way.

At the other end of the big room was another table of boys that were eyeing my table as if they wanted to break us into a million pieces. Suddenly wanting to get out of there, I checked my watch, 7:56, Oh god, I needed to go to power class or I would be late.

CHAPTER 7

Rick, my new master, was really cool. He provoked us, so we would use Electricity. Then he gave us a small light bulb and told us that if we get angry, we should try and light it up. I bet José five bucks that I could light it up at least four times as soon as I talked to Grace after the lesson.

Then Rick wanted to see how fast we ran. I found out that now that I had my Power I could run ten times faster than normal when using my Power. When I told Rick this, he said after all our training we could all run as fast as it takes for a light to turn on when you flick the switch. That's really fast, in case you didn't get that.

History of Powers class was really boring. All the kids from all the forms of 9-1 were there. Bob, the master of this class, ran up and down the aisle and sung babyish songs, getting looks that said: It's not like we're six, *geez* . . .

Math and English were the same as on Earth. You could not use your Power in them. And there were about four different forms and about twenty kids, all about my age.

Lunch was about the same as breakfast. Break was fun. John, Jose, Sam, and I went to the dueling ring and watched kids try and beat each other up for a half an hour. The matches were all scheduled on a board next to a sign up sheet. That would explain the older kids' looks. I guessed any serious arguments were dealt with here, the moves looked like they came out of a movie, or more importantly they were like the ones I'd seen my sister use on a guy who was bullying Jake last year. The kid was in the hospital for a month.

In gym there were only three Powers that Electricity couldn't outrun, Light, Air, and Super Speed. That's all we really did, run.

Karate was just blocks and stances, except at the end of the hour we got to punch and kick punching bags while the masters walked around correcting our techniques and giving helpful advice.

During the second break, things got exciting. My form met up with the full group and we were lounging in a room off to the side of the dueling room for kids, waiting for a fight, but anyone can relax in there. So while we were just sitting there minding our own business, the boys I saw at breakfast came over. They stood in a 'V' shape. A really mean looking older guy stood at the front. Black saggy hair, black eyes and pale skin defined him as having Darkness. His friends were all older than me and all looked mean.

"Okay, you older ones get out of the way so I can teach the little ones whose da boss." The big one growled, making a big Darkness ball in his hand. With that, Grant stepped in front of me.

"There's nothing you can do to me, Ripper." He said calmly, looking at the Darkness ball.

"With this I can't. Here Link, catch." Throwing the Darkness ball behind him, it hit his green-eyed Plant friend who fell unconscious, almost immediately. Suddenly Ripper balled his fist and thrust it in to my brother's stomach. Grant went flying into the wall where he lay moaning. Ripper and his cronies strutted away.

As soon as Ripper was gone, we hurried to Grant's aid.

"Ugh. Ripper is such a *ss." Grant grimaced as Grace checked him for broken bones.

"Looks like you're clear Grant, but I wouldn't move just to be sure." Grace said, "Scar, I thought I saw your brother in the dueling room, can you have him brought to the infirmary?"

Scarlett nodded and stuck her head into the dueling room door, "Jasper, *Grant è ferito. Potresti portarlo in infermeria?*" Scarlett spoke in a different language.

"Italian. She's from Venice." Grace explained.

A guy walked in, he looked like an older male version of Scarlett but with a gentler jaw line and purple eyes: Psychic.

"Hi Jasper, you don't need to help. I can go to the infirmary myself." Grant said, obviously trying to save face in front of the older guy.

"That's not smart," he said simply. With a flick of his wrist Grant jumped off the ground and levitated in midair. Once Grant was steady Jasper walked off towards the medical center with my floating brother in tow.

Okay, so life wasn't going to be so boring after all.

CHAPTER 8

Two months had passed since I first arrived at JAP. Things had really progressed. I could make, control, and was working on sucking up Electricity. I became a yellow belt in basic karate at the end of the two months. I was now taking part in my siblings' fights, two against one of free-for-all, which wasn't necessary a good thing, but an accomplishment, nonetheless.

One day in History of Powers Class, we were learning about rare Powers. Bob was talking about the rarest Power in the Power based world, Body. Those who get Body are at least fifty years apart in age. Apparently it was forty-nine years since the last Body got their Power, so a new kid should get Body soon.

As Bob said this, I thought he looked right at me, but he looked away so fast that I started to think I had just imagined it. He went on to say that the last Body was a girl so the next one should be a boy. This time I saw a meaningful glance my way. It was as if Bob wanted me to take a hint, but I didn't know where or how to take it.

Bob went on and on about how those with Body were stronger, faster, and smarter than the Power human, with a few exceptions, as well as had the ability to heal others and themselves. They also lived longer than anyone in known history. Every time Bob told us one of these facts, he would look right at me for abut half a second with a pointed expression on his face. When I told Grant and Grace, they didn't understand the looks either, but agreed that they meant something.

J   J   J   J   J

The next morning, at breakfast, John came up to my siblings and me.

"My granddad told me to tell you three that he wants to see you in his office. The Goes code is O-001. Don't ask me what he wants, but I think you guys have a mission." I had completely forgotten that John's grandfather was the headmaster here.

As I typed in the code to the Goes I wondered what awaited us.

CHAPTER 9

John's grandpa looked like a stereotypical grandfather with a thin layer of white hair lain over his round face. The only thing wrong with the picture was the worried frown, creating wrinkles on his forehead.

"Kids, I have bad news and good news, you pick," he said.

"Good," Grant said timidly.

"You're going on a mission," said the Headmaster.

"Okay, now bad." Grace said, flinching.

"Your younger brother is in danger. I'm sending you three back to earth for a week to transfer him over to adults."

"Well, what are we waiting for?!" yelled Grace. She was getting angry; a watery blue color was spilling into the whites of her eyes. Seeing this I backed away. The angrier she was, the more chance of me going for an unexpected swim.

"Your acceptance." said the headmaster. I don't know how he could be so calm.

"Yes, okay, *let's* go!" shrieked Grace.

"Grace, I meant all three of you," he told her.

"I'm in." I said immediately. Jake, in trouble? Don't try and keep me away.

"Do you really have to ask?" Grant said.

All right, tell anyone who asks, we have a fall break. Stick to Jake and your room most of the time, but I want hourly patrols. Act like you're out for a walk. In general, avoid confrontation. Now I'd prefer if you all wear formal uniforms, they provide extra padding." The Headmaster said, looking from blue eyes to black then to hazel. As he gazed at me, I was with Jake at the orphanage. Jake was crying out for Grace, Grant, and me. Just as he said my name, there was a knock at the door, and Jake went and hid in the closet.

I suddenly realized that this was just an Illusion trick, but I felt that what I was being shown was real.

"You have Illusion." I whispered, still shaken by the vision of Jake.

"Indeed." The headmaster snapped his fingers, and suddenly looming in front of us was the biggest Goes ever. It could have held fifty kids in it at once.

Grace, Grant, and I got in.

CHAPTER 10

On the bus, which was now a normal bus, I told my siblings what the Headmaster had shown me. Grace looked like she wanted to fly to earth and give Jake a hug but of course we were in space so that couldn't happen.

"You know, somebody told me that if you complete a mission you get something cool for your room." Grant told me about fifteen minutes into the five hour trip. At this Grace slapped his face.

"Our brother is in danger or dying or worse and all you can think of is which new game station you're going to get out of this?!" There was literally steam coming out of her ears. It reminded me so much of a cartoon that I had to struggle not to laugh.

"Okay, okay! Sorry. That was stupid. I wasn't thinking!" Grant pulled himself into a corner of the seat and built a protective shield of darkness around himself. Grace huffed off and sat in a seat on the other side of the bus to look out the window.

An hour in, frustrated by waiting, I did what we people with Powers tend to do when we need to pass the time. We rough-house, with the emphasis on *rough*. I challenged Grant to a one on one face off, since the bus driver let us out of our seats once we were in space.

"Sorry Jess, but I'm a green belt in karate, and frankly I move just as fast as you." Grant said as he jumped over my head.

"How are you as fast as me when I move the speed of light and you move."

"The speed of light, too. You move as fast as electricity and I move as fast as darkness," he said, throwing a darkness ball at me.

"Which is slow, right?" I said jumping up on the back of the seat to keep myself from getting hurt.

"No, I move as fast as it takes to turn off a light." He said as he swung himself over the back of the seat in front of me. He kicked me in the chest so I fell backward landing on the cold plastic floor. Trapped in the place where people put their feet, I was a sitting duck for my brother's attacks. I tried to get up. Epic failure. Grant perched on the seat back above me.

"Now, now, Jessica." He smiled, relishing the moment. Grace was always protecting anyone who was being attacked, usually with one of her own . . . But seeing as she was giving us the silent treatment . . .

"Don't struggle and this won't hurt a bit." He said as a growing darkness ball formed in his hands. Just as I made my final struggle, Grant playfully dropped the ball of anti-matter.

As the anti-matter made contact, I discovered a new feeling. It wasn't the burn water made, it was sharper. It felt like all my energy was draining out of me.

"Oops, I lied. It hurts like crazy even if you don't struggle."

Somehow, using the pain and anger, I was able to get up and slam my older brother into the seat five rows in front of us. But I wasn't done there; I had to send him into a sparking seizure.

"*Grace, help!*" She raised her hand leisurely and blasted me away from our brother. I got a glimpse of myself in the rearview mirror. My eyes were not hazel, but yellow, that seemed to be fading away as did my anger. I had used too much of my Power, so when I hit the window. I passed out.

J   J   J   J   J

When I woke up, the bus was an airplane and was looking for a place to land just outside of Manhattan. I had a massive headache which figures; I had been smashed against a wall. Grant was putting on sunscreen because even the October sun could burn him. Grace was anxiously helping the driver look for a place to land. Out the window were the nighttime lights of the city that I had once called home. Over past few months, J.A.P. had become my home to the point where New York was more like the home of a close friend or a favorite relative. I knew my way around and was more than comfortable here. But if anyone asked me where home was, I would picture my dorm and the classroom of J.A.P. not the orphanage.

I could feel the lights as they flicked on. As we landed we set up patrol shifts.

"I'll take midnight. Grant, you take one in the morning, and Jess, you take two. I'll go after that and we'll go on like that. We each get eight shifts." Grace was really nervous, and for obvious reasons. Not only was our younger brother in danger, but also we had no idea what we needed to protect him from.

We were dropped off across town from St. Mary's Orphanage. For a few minutes we all just stood there, acclimating ourselves to the surroundings. Earth was literally a totally different planet from Jupiter. A bus passing by caused all of us to jump; and Grant had to cover his mouth to keep himself from screaming like a little girl when a pigeon landed nearby.

Finally, we came to our senses and Grace hailed a taxi.

CHAPTER 11

Outside St. Mary's we made plans about our entry into our orphanage room so that we wouldn't be seen or cause unwanted questions. Or should I say Grace made plans.

"Since it's night, Grant, go up through the darkness. Jess, run up but pleeeaase be careful. We already have one sibling to save. Then turn on the water, and I'll be up in a minute." Grace said.

I ran through the open door. It was a rush. I dodged and jumped, but I wasn't ever noticed. I realized that I was moving ten times faster than I used to when I slammed into the door of my family's room. I burst in and sprinted to the bathroom, turned on the water in the sink, and ran back to where Jake was hiding in the corner.

"I don't have a Power. Please don't hurt me again." Jake was crying. *Again? Who had got here before us?* I knelt down to take my little brother's hand. I'd never seen him so scared before. Why oh why did I leave him?

"Jake, it's me, Jess. And—." I started to say.

"Grant," said a voice to my left.

"And Grace," she said, as she walked out of the bathroom.

"And Chester, Ike, and Conner," rumbled a voice behind me.

We turned around as the lights flicked on. Three heavily built boys stood in a line against the far wall. All of them wore jumpsuits with nametags and the letters S.A.P.T. Grace walked swiftly over to them and looked at their nametags. For some reason they didn't attack her, maybe they wanted to intimidate us into letting them hurt our brother. *Like that was going to work.*

"F12-5, that's Fire, and you're Chester." She doused his red hair as it ignited. "I12-6, judging by your pale blue eyes, that's Ice, Ike." He froze her hand, but Grace slugged him in the shoulder. "And Conner, S12-4, that's—."

Just then a big wolf leaped up at her. Its claws raked her cheek. Grace wiped her hand across the wound, and then shot bloody water at both wolf-Conner and Chester. Ike tried to get at Jake during the commotion, but Grant met him with a kick to the stomach. Now snake-Conner attempted to attack Grace again. *Attempted.* I got to him first and backed him up to the window by using his animal instincts against him. Sparking him, as he switched forms, we exchanged attacks.

Just as we reached the window, I made the mistake of throwing a punch at Conner; he was expecting that and ducked under it. The glass shattered on my arm just by the elbow. Blood started to gush out of the wound. I wanted to cry, but I remembered from one of my karate classes: *Don't show fear or pain; if you do your enemy can use that against you.* Conner took the moment to run for the bathroom.

I looked around the room for my siblings. Grace was nowhere to be seen, but there was steam coming out of the closet so she had probably fallen in while fighting Chester. Grant was frozen in a block of ice and Ike was on floor having his energy sucked into a darkness ball on his leg. Jake was hiding in his bed, which was by the bathroom. Conner was headed straight at Jake! I had to stop him.

I made a running jump off Grant's bed and landed on Conner. There was a dull thud as his head hit the ground. The speed of my attack caught Conner off guard; he had no time to change forms.

"Grace, you okay?" I called. Grace, being the oldest, had the most responsibility. She would want to know everything that had happened in the fight.

"Yeah, I couldn't stop Chester from burning through my best dress here, but other than that I'm fine." She stepped out of the closet.

As Grace started to thaw out Grant, I spotted a bad burn on her right hand, but when she saw me looking she put the hand in her pocket. I wrapped the ice on Grant's shoulder; I hadn't realized that blood had seeped down my arm till there was blood on the ice.

"Jess! Your arm is covered in blood. Here, I'll clean it up." Grace yelped. She ran to the bathroom and came back with one of those wipes made by Oxiclean.

"Wait, that has water in it!" I cried as I pulled my arm away.

"Oh right, sorry. Here I'll suck the water up off your arm as I clean up the blood." This was one of Grace's more motherly traits.

I stuck out my arm and let her get to work, first wiping off the blood, which hurt as the water touched my skin, and then wrapping the cut in gauze. The actual injury, without the blood on my arm, was about an inch long and half an inch wide.

After she had wrapped my wound, Grace went back to unfreezing Grant. I didn't need to be there for that so I walked over to Jake. He was pretty much in shock. A six year old wasn't supposed to see that kind of violence. A hug seemed to calm him down a little, but I don't think he liked seeing the unconscious bodies around the room. So as soon as Grant was moving again, the three of us pulled the three boys out to the fire escape and dropped them.

Then, much the worse for wear, and covered head to toe in soot, water, burns, and cuts, we gathered around our baby brother and tried to console him. I think though, that our appearances pretty much counteracted anything we said in the way of "you don't have to worry, they'll never hurt you again." I mean, seriously, if a bunch of scared, injured kids informed you that they would protect you from everything, how much of it would you believe?

CHAPTER 12

Throughout the next week, Grace, Grant, and I were on guard. When Jake was in the building we did patrols, walking every hallway and around the building. When Jake was not in the building, but at school, we followed him like hawks, and hid in our various ways out of sight of any normal human.

A week after our arrival, I was sitting on the fire escape eating some chicken I stole from the kitchen, watching the sunset behind the buildings. Just as the street lamps came on, I heard a growl from above me. I looked and saw a lion, its teeth bared and its blue eyes filled with hate. *Wait, blue eyes? I though lions had greenish yellow eyes . . .* then it hit me . . . It was Conner.

Just as I realized this, lion-Conner jumped off the roof and slammed his front paws into my side, knocking me over the edge. I would have been a Jessica pancake if I didn't grab the ladder to the ground. Conner then became a monkey and climbed down after me. As soon as he reached the ground, he turned back into a lion. I tried to run away, but I tripped on a garbage bag. My foot kicked the dumpster, and another bag fell on my left arm, I was trapped!

Conner, still a lion, looked at me like he was wondering whether he should bite my head off, literally, but then he got an evil gleam in his eye. I think he thought of a more painful way for me to die.

He leaped into the air, roaring, changed into a bear and fell on my right arm. I heard the sickening snap, but only felt the pain for a second. Then, some mix of anger, fear, and just pure adrenaline hit my brain and that was it. Suddenly my left hand found a knife in the bag.

As I spun around to face my attacker, I glanced at the fire escape, and had to suppress a bust of laughter at Grace running down so fast that she tripped over every other step. Just as I cleared my head, a black-red-and-yellow snake rose into my line of vision. Its fang must have been the length of my arms, and I shuddered to think what kinds of horrible poisons would be put into my body should I lose this fight.

Suddenly, three different things happened at the same time: snake-Conner bit my right arm, I stabbed him in the back, and Grace screamed my name. My vision blurred as Grace jumped the last floor and ran over.

"Jess! Jess stay with me! Please, please, please!" Grace half cried, half screamed. "Grant, call the Headmaster, now!"

Grant poked his head out the door, nodded, and disappeared back into the orphanage. Now my vision was swimming in and out of focus. I *was* trying to 'stay with' Grace, but I just couldn't. I felt all of my muscles failing me. I had to try one last time to look at Grace before I died.

My eyes met my sister's for the split second before they closed.

CHAPTER 13

My first sensation was a feeling that told me that if I didn't itch my right arm right then, well, I didn't know what I would do. That's how bad it was. Slowly, I made my left hand obey me and brought it across my body, but my fingernails met plaster. This was wrong. My muddled brain struggled to figure out what was going on. At first I thought that my arm was totally gone, as I groped around in the space I somehow knew it would be. Suddenly, I found my fingertip, and realized that my arm was in a cast. Slowly, I swam out of my daze. I felt the pillow under my head, and a quick blink of my eye forced me to close them even tighter than ever. The lights were soooo bright.

Suddenly I heard footsteps. "Jess, can you hear me?" a voice said to my right.

Then a sigh came from my left. "You've been asking her that for the past six days. She doesn't hear you."

For a minute, I struggled in confusion. I *knew* those voices. They were so familiar. Then, I realized that I recognized both voices, Grace and Grant! But how were they here? Those fangs! And the pain! A weird collage of feelings and memories was coming over me. I had thought for sure that . . . but if they were here then . . . I wasn't dead or out cold! This thought made me fight even harder against the sleep that I could feel coming over me.

"Actually Grant, I can hear both of you." I corrected. My voice sounded strange. Muddled and slurred. I was soooo tired . . . but I had to see them . . . make sure they were really there as I opened my eyes to look at my older brother.

"Jess! You're awake! First, you went all pale and didn't respond to anything. Then when the medic bus finally came they took forever to actually treat you. They kept asking questions about Conner and you. Then they had to get the antidote to the poison, and by then you had been out of like five minutes. The head medic told us to tell Jake we were leaving . . ." She paused trying to catch her breath. "When we got here you didn't wake up and they didn't know if you ever would. And . . . and . . . yeah. So um . . . yeah."

My head hurt from so much noise. But I couldn't help but smile. This was definitely Grant. Talking way too fast, like there was some sort of endless race on, and then faltering at the end when he got to the part about his feelings. I knew what he was saying though. That he had been worried. And that he loved me. Not, of course, that he ever would have said that to my face. Besides that, only one part of that story popped in my mind, "You left Jake, alone, on Earth, with Chester and Ike STILL OUT THERE!" *I almost gave up my life for that boy and they just throw it away?*

"Yes . . . I mean no. We only left 'cause you were hurt and the headmaster told us S.A.P.T. gave up." Grace was unsuccessfully trying to stop my anger. "Conner only stayed to get revenge."

I managed to get out of bed and walk toward the exit defiantly, my newfound fury overpowering my tiredness and pain.

"Wait, you're not fully healed." Grace got up to stop me, but I wacked my plastered arm against her chest knocking her into Grant.

I stumbled into the Goes punched in the code for my room. I needed some time alone.

J   J   J   J   J

Once I got to my room, my full anger broke loose. I was so upset that I didn't stop thrashing around till I zapped my rug and set it on fire.

As I stomped it out, I was suddenly exhausted. I could barely even hold my head up! How hadn't I realized this before? I collapsed onto my bed and suddenly it hit me. I wasn't as mad at Grace or Grant as I was with myself. Of course, I just *had* to be the strong one and fight Conner. Why am I such an activist, always running into fights I can't win?

What I really needed was to find some company to get my mind off Jake. So I headed to the dueling room to see whom I could find.

CHAPTER 14

I found Dani and Samantha watching Esmeralda bash up the Johnson twins: Robert and James.

"Hey guys!" I called out, running over to them.

"Hey Jess, how you doing?" Dani said, not really paying attention to me. "Get James, Ezzy! What's up, Jess?"

"I'll bet you guys five bucks that my family is more messed up then yours." I sat down in between Sam and Dani.

Dani winced a little, and Sam turned around, smiling. "I won't take that bet. My mom has Air and so does my brother. He's twenty. My dad has Electricity like me. What about you, Dani?"

"Um . . . well . . . um . . ." She seemed to be looking for a way out of answering but I couldn't imagine why. *What was so bad about her family? At least she probably had one that wasn't constantly fighting and running away from unimaginable dangers.* As soon as I thought this I hated myself for it. At least I had a family that loved and supported each other, in our own little ways. Which sure was more that I could say for a lot of the kids here.

Finally, some part of her inner struggle won, and she turned to me, giving me her full attention. "My mom divorced my dad when she found out he had a Power. She's a regular human and he has Water. My brother and sister are duds. He's sixteen and she's fourteen. When I got my Power, my dad got all my stuff and moved it to his house." She blurted it out so fast that I could barely understand what she was saying, and then turned away.

She looked so sad, I wanted to comfort her but I didn't know how. I didn't want to give her the five bucks because I didn't want to tell her that I thought that her family was more messed up than mine. It just didn't seem right. So we just sat there in awkward silence till Scarlett walked over.

"Hey Scarlett," I asked innocently. "What's your family like?"

Tommy Wood was walking by and heard what I had asked. "Scarlett just loves to talk about her big caring family." I could tell that he was joking but Scarlett took it the wrong way.

"Shut up, Tommy" she said through gritted teeth.

"Hey, it's not my fault Stella-" Wham! Scarlett had coated her right hand in Darkness and slapped Tommy in the face with it. She continued to punch and kick him, while yelling and shouting in Italian, none of which sounded too nice.

Grant, who had just entered the room, ran over to me. "Did you say the 'F' word?"

"I don't curse!" I whispered indignantly. I didn't know what I had said, but I was petrified that I might become Scarlett's next punching bag.

Grant rolled his dark eyes, "I meant 'Family.'" He walked down the aisle and pulled Scarlett off Tommy.

"Come on, Scarlett. He was only teasing," he said, soothingly.

Scarlett didn't answer, her eyes bulged out of her head and she flailed at Tommy. Eventually but she stopped fighting. She shook Grant off and stomped out of the room.

"What's so bad about saying 'family'?" asked Samantha.

"Usually, nothing. But in front of Scarlett, many things." said Tommy, picking himself off the floor gingerly and holding up his battered arm for all to see.

"Like what?" Dani stood up and walked over to Tommy to examine his arm.

"Well, she has a twin sister, Stella. Just don't mention her in front of Scarlett." Grant said rapping his knuckles on Tommy's head and playfully shoved him back a few steps.

"Why?" I inquired.

Ezmerelda walked over, dragging the bedraggled two twin boys she had been fighting, James and Robert. "Why what?"

"Why not mention Stella in front of Scarlett?" Samantha filled her in.

"Oh because Scarlett will get really angry. That's like, the *only* thing that makes her lose her temper."

"Wait, if Scarlett never talks about Stella, then how do you know?" Dani asked.

"We had a sleepover and um . . . she talks in her sleep." Ezmerelda said. At this, Grant and Tommy snickered. "Hey, Sean, let's go!" Ezzy's Metal boyfriend, Sean de Hierro, was walking over to take her to the dating spot: the place where the sun is always setting, but never actually sets. If you asked me, it was all a little cliché and cheesy, but on a planet severely lacking in diners and bowling alleys, we took what we could get. Still, I couldn't help rolling my eyes as Ezmerelda jumped into her twelve year old boyfriend's arms. She waved to us as they left.

"Hey, Jess, you should talk to your master to find out what you missed," called Grant as he walked away with his friends. A couple of them laughed and said something about turning me into a good-goody. Grant chuckled and elbowed them playfully in the stomach.

CHAPTER 15

Grace was walking out of the infirmary rubbing the band-aid on her forehead, as Jess was heading to the library. Grace could still see the anger in her little sister's eyes. She knew that another encounter with Jess now would only set her off more.

She ducked back into the doorway, her long blue hair trailing out behind her. It began to curl and blow around her, like it did every time she was agitated. Sometimes her hair just plainly freaked her out. She still wasn't used to the vibrant color, and the way it reacted to her feelings had almost led her to shave it off after an especially bad fight with Jess.

As soon as Grace made it to the Goes, she broke down. She had had a very bad last two weeks. Between Jess and Jake's near death experiences, she was stretched to the limit. On top of that was the fact that now Jessica hated her. Why was she the *only* one trying to keep this family together? Oh yeah, and Peter would never love her. Grace knew she had to get a hold of herself. She took a few deep breaths and stepped into the dining hall just as the last strand of her wild mane settled down on her shoulders.

"Where's . . ." She hadn't even finished her sentence. At least three people turned and shouted something at her.

Confused, she sat down and looked at a now calm Scarlett to clarify. "In the library. Something about peace, quiet, and an essay due tomorrow." Scarlett gave Grace a sympathetic look as Ezmerelda sat down next to them, and picked at her salad and french-fries. Grace and Peter turned and shot each other looks. Uh oh, break up food. This would be a rough evening.

"What's wrong Ezzy?" Hannah asked, a look of concern on her face. Grace had to stifle a laugh at Hannah's cluelessness.

"S-Sean dumped me." Behind Esmeralda a group of boys had stopped what they were doing and a few of them started making flowers and handing them out to their friends.

"Um, Ezzy, turn around." Dani, who had never been there when Ezmerelda had had a break-up, was staring at these boys, but Grace knew who they were. This group waited, chomping at the bit for Ezmerelda to break up with whatever guy she was with and then heal her heart and pamper her so she would date one of them.

After watching this group drool over her friend for a while, Grace changed seats to sit next to Peter. She thought she saw a smile pass over his face, but she probably just wanted it to be there. *Ugh.* But this was better than going back to the dorm and facing Jess.

CHAPTER 16

"Sally, I don't care if you're mentoring his wife. I'm not going to mentor Camden. He fights like a eight week old," Andrew Clease said as he hung up on his wife. He always used the eight-week-old jest because that was how old each of his three youngest kids had been when they were sent to the orphanage in New York. At nineteen he had to give up his one-year-old daughter and eight week old son. A year later, a girl of again eight weeks was handed over to the orphanage staff, three years later a final boy. Sally and he had told the orphanage that they couldn't take care of them. It killed him that they had to be sent away, but it was for their protection. As far as they knew, he and his wife were dead.

Speaking of the kids, I should check and see if Hodd sent me any emails about them. He typed 'children' into the email search of his laptop. Two emails came up, one said that his third-born, Jessica, had received her Power, Electricity. The other said she'd been sent on a mission with her older siblings, Grace and Grant. The mission was to protect his youngest son Jake, but Jessica had her arm broken by a shape-shifter who also gave her a snakebite.

Surprised and horrified, he shut his laptop, just as a loud bang went off in the waiting room. Andrew looked up and across the dueling room where he relaxed. Probably just some crazy kids, he thought as he put his computer away. Then again, it was almost two and even Mentors like himself knew that students were meant to be in class. Something was up.

Andrew put his computer away and looked at the door only to see a young girl slam into the window. He didn't see her face but he did see the vines wrapped around her waist.

He was half way down the bleachers, when she was thrown to the ceiling as the vines unraveled from her waist. Screaming, she tumbled towards the floor. At the door, an explosion slammed her back to the ceiling. Inside the room now, a teenager ran at her falling form and he smashed the girl into the wall with his oncoming shoulder.

Horrified, Andrew ran down across the room as six burly kids with greased hair and grimy uniforms joined the similarly dressed teen in a huddle around the girl. They laughed and kicked her as she moaned. "Boys aren't you meant to be in class?" Andrew's appearance made them jump out of their skins. One look at his blue nametag told them he was a mentor, and not one to get into a fight with.

"Guys, lets get out of here." The largest boy yelled. He was dark haired and dark eyed, but his skin was pearly white. Andrew balked slightly as he recognized the traits of Darkness.

He watched them run until the last one had disappeared into the Goes. Then he turned to the girl on the floor. Her blond hair covered her head and shoulders, as she lay unconscious on the hard floor. Andrew rolled her over to inspect how badly she had been injured. Never in his wildest dreams did he expect to see what he did.

From the many pictures of his children that he received from the headmaster, Andrew knew what his children looked like even though he hadn't seen them since they were babies. Jessica Clease, his daughter! Just to be sure, he checked her nametag. There it was, Jessica Clease: USA E9-1.

"Who is she?" Andrew's best friend and brother-in-law Michael Comuz had just come up behind him.

"My . . . my daughter." Andrew was in shock. He knew that he wasn't supposed to have any contact with his children until his youngest child received his Power. Everything had been planned so that even though he worked at her school, she would never come into contact with him or Sally by mistake. Yet here she was in his arms. He knew that he couldn't reveal himself to her, but it was a comfort to at least see her, at last.

"I didn't know I had a niece." Michael mused. "Thanks for telling me bro."

"You have two nieces and two nephews. This is Jessica, my third-born. They don't know me or Sally, and Hodd wants it to stay that way till the youngest, Jake, gets his Power." Andrew said sternly, he would not go against the Headmaster's orders.

"Andy, chill, I won't tell her if she wakes up. Here, I'll take her back to her dorm for you. You shouldn't be with her when she wakes up" Mike thumped him on the shoulder. Andrew knew he was right, and he wouldn't dream of disobeying the headmaster, but every atom in his body fought against the idea. His daughter was here, after all these years and he wanted to keep the moment as long as he could.

He was about to complain but just then Jessica's eyes fluttered open. A hand flew to her right arm, which Andy just noticed was in a cast.

"What happened?" Mike said with an uncle-like concern.

"A mission. Did you see which way the gang that knocked me out went? I want to head them off. If they think they can rough me around because I went on a mission and broke my arm, they've got another thing coming." She growled, and some dormant paternal instinct kicked in somewhere inside Andrew.

"No, you're in no shape to go picking fights. How and why did you get yourself into that one with those boys?" Andrew *was* proud that she wanted to redeem herself, but it was just plain dumb to go pick fights when you can't win.

Jessica sighed. "I will get them for this, this is the last time Ripper's gang wins a fight against me," she vowed. "I was just watching TV 'cause I can't go to gym, and they come and pick on me." Her voice was defensive, but Andrew doubted that was how it happened, it rarely was at J.A.P.

"Do you want me to walk you home? You hit your head pretty hard." A few more minutes with a daughter he never got to truly meet would make his day.

"Uh . . . If you don't mind." She said to Andrew, suddenly sheepish.

Andrew quickly told Michael that they'd meet up later and shot him a meaningful glance before he could protest. Then he put his daughter's arm around his shoulders for support and brought her home.

CHAPTER 17

Several months passed quickly, the time marked only by holidays. Halloween was sick. Imagine over one thousand kids in costume running over twenty six dorm rooms, in a building, maybe fifteen stories high. At breakfast that morning, Hodd (did I ever tell you the headmaster's name was Hodd? It's kind of odd, get it?) explained the concept of Halloween and its history. When I asked Grace, why didn't every one know about my favorite holiday, she said that most of the world didn't celebrate it. *Who knew? They miss all that candy? Not me.*

Thanksgiving was lame. The Americans got turkey for dinner, but that was about it.

Christmas. Epic. I was raised in a Christian orphanage, but Christmas without grown-ups was 'da bomb'! Decorated trees everywhere, and lights in every room and hallway.

Scarlett and Dani had to be forced home for winter break.

New Year's was a cross between Halloween and Thanksgiving. Not everyone celebrates it on Jupiter, but more people celebrate it than Thanksgiving. Anyway, we had a party in our dorm, dancing to a playlist: Avril Lavigne, Green Day, and Owl City. Grace and Peter got together, finally. That was my doing. I told Grace that Peter liked her in the middle of Avril Lavigne's *Fall to Pieces*. I think that was good planning on my part, if I do say so myself. They slow danced to Owl City's *Vanilla Twilight*.

We celebrated Esmeralda's twelfth birthday on the fifth of January.

When Scarlett and Dani came back to school, Scarlett had new cuts and scars and Dani was in low spirits. They didn't explain, but then again, they really didn't need to.

My run in with Ripper's gang and Conner taught me one thing: I wasn't skilled enough! If I wanted to live up to my own standards, I needed to put my heart and soul into my training.

After I made that commitment and my cast was taken off, I achieved my orange belt, then red. In three months! My gym teacher said that I could run across the US in fifty seconds. Not that I would get to test that any time soon being 500 million miles away from Earth.

In December, I asked Rick what I could do to get *really* strong and he gave me an anatomy book to study. Every muscle in the body was described in great detail and their uses listed. He said that if I could have better control over more muscles, then my body would react better to any signals my brain sent.

J   J   J   J   J

Hodd sat at his desk. The fifty-one year old man looked at a picture and his eyes filled up with tears. It was the anniversary of the saddest two days of Hodd's life. Nineteen years before, his younger brother died in a car crash leaving Hodd with his brother's thirteen-year-old son, Daniel. The boy, full of anger, irrationally blamed his uncle for the accident, and thirteen years later he changed his last name to Sapt, killed the family controlling the school, and took over everything, using his incredibly strong Powers to silence any protestors.

Then just eleven years and a day after his bother died, Hodd lost his only son and daughter-in-law to Daniel and his students. Hodd raised their seven-year-old daughter,

Leah, and her one-year-old brother, John, by himself because his wife had left long ago.

Leah walked into the room and sat on his desk. Usually she was out with friends, but today she knew that she was more needed here.

"Morning, granddad." she said softly.

She remembered her parents well and judging by the red around her eyes she had been crying. He gave her a shaky smile, unable to speak through the lump in his throat.

Suddenly his granddaughter burst into tears. "Oh Grandad" she hiccupped between sobs. "Why?! Oh it's not supposed to be like this! I want my daddy and mommy back! I want to hear their voices, and, and, *hic* and, and I want them to hold me and tell me that they love me, *hic, hic*, oh! Do you know what I said to them, Grandad; the last time I saw them? I told them that I hated them and I wished they would *die!!!* Oh god, all because they wouldn't let me go to a movie with my friends on a school night. And I never *hic* I never ever ever get to take it back now. They're gone!!!!!!!! *Hic hic hic. I wanna kill him, slo-hic-ly and PAINFULLY! Hic hic hic hic . . ."*

He held her until her sobs became sniffles. "Oh sweetie, they knew you loved them, just like they loved . . ." Just then a message came up on his phone: *Jake Clease is in red alarm again. Get siblings on the bus ASAP.* Oh no.

"Leah, can you call a friend or talk to your brother? I have to attend to this."

"You're just ditching me? *Now*?" She looked heartbroken.

"This boy could very well be your key to getting at Daniel and now he's in danger. I have to get his older siblings there fast. I'm sorry."

"Go," she sniffed, "it's-*hic*-okay I'll talk to John."

"Thank you."

He knocked on the Clease dorm door five minutes later. Grant opened the door; behind him Hodd could see the girls on the ground fighting.

"Oh, hi ***Hodd***." The boy said his headmaster's name a little louder than the rest of his sentence.

The fight stopped in its tracks, Jessica with a long twist of her older sister's hair wound around her hand, Grace with her nails half way down Jessica's right cheek.

"Jake's in danger, get into your formal wear," He said.

"Again?" Jessica whined.

"Your brother is destined to get a very special Power and everyone wants to harness it. When the people after him find that he doesn't have it yet, they *will* kill him." Hodd told them. He conveniently forgot to mention that it was Daniel behind the attacks on Jake. That wasn't exactly going to boost their morale. After all, the less scared they were going into this, the better chance they had, he hoped.

"Okay, okay, we'll get ready and be at the buses in five. Right guys?" Jessica said.

When her siblings nodded, Hodd left to arrange for the bus.

CHAPTER 18

"Jess, quit bouncing, I keep thinking you're, like, fighting someone," Grace said. It was true. I was jumping up and down like a ball.

"I can't help it! I'm so nervous," I responded, glancing around suspiciously at all the parents and babysitters standing outside Jake's school with us.

Grace was just as jumpy as I was, but she didn't jump, she just switched her position every other second. In sharp contrast, Grant was just leaning against the brick wall, calm as a lake on a windless day.

Finally, after what seemed like ages, the kids began to trickle out of the big double doors, and then they flew out in a rush, talking and shouting and playing. Several of them climbed into the orphanage van, and Grace followed them to talk to the driver about letting Jake walk home with us.

When she returned several minutes later, Jake still hadn't appeared. We waited, getting more and more nervous by the second. The orphanage van left and an identical one pulled up in the same place. Jake was finally pushing out the door with the last stragglers, and we saw him walk towards the van. Too late, I realized what was going on, and I went running and screaming towards him. He climbed in the door and I saw his muscles tense in surprise. He tried to step back, but it was too late. The van was pulling away too fast for him to get out. Caught in the dust and exhaust behind it, I saw the shape of an arm and hand, covered in black, reach out and slam the swinging door.

"Get that van," Grant yelled. Without another word to each other we were off like rockets.

We chased that van for what seemed like forever before Grant grasped the back door and pull Grace and me on with him. Climbing on top, I grabbed onto the rack with one hand and swung Grace up with the other. Grant began to work on unhinging the doors.

It was slow work, and Grace seemed to quickly lose patience. Looking over the edge of the van, she must have spotted her opportunity because she swung herself around like a monkey into the open passenger side window.

Shaking and swerving violently, our metal horse threatened to topple over and crush us, and we lost no time following our sister's lead.

The next couple seconds was a blur of limbs. Suddenly I was hitting the back wall, and watched as a man shut a plastic screen. I looked around, Grant was nursing a cut arm and Jake seemed fine, but scared. Grace lay still in the corner. Her head was bleeding. I crawled over. Without saying a word to my brothers I moved her so I could hold her close.

We sat in silence for hours, before falling asleep. We didn't feel the car stop, or feel people pick us up.

I did however hear a man say, "She's cute." A second voice responded, "Yeah, too bad Daniel . . ." and then I blacked out again before I could hear the rest.

CHAPTER 19

When I awoke in the morning, I was in a cell, the kind that I assumed they used for prisoners in real life but had only seen in movies. A metal toilet, metal sink, and two metal bunk beds were one continuous solid piece connected by a solid metal floor. Two scratchy black blankets on each bunk added to the décor.

Groaning I sat up as upright as the big bruises covering my back would allow. I was attempting to brush my hair with my fingers, when a tall woman walked in. She had red hair and visible muscles. I would have thought her pretty except for a large, perfectly circular scar disfiguring half of her forehead.

"Ya like ma scar, lil' girl? Well ya can have one just like it if yer good." Her voice was gruff. She didn't wait for an answer, turning to my siblings and throwing them roughly onto the floor.

Once we all stood up, she led us into another room with about six men waiting. We were briskly cuffed and then Jake was shoved into the center of the room. They poked and stabbed him, injecting him with bits of their Powers to see what he was immune too. Grace screamed and tried to wriggle free to get to him, but three men the size of bears pinned her against a wall. By the end of the whole ordeal, my little brother was curled up in a ball, screaming in pain.

"Okay, he's got no Power. What are we gonna do with them, *what are we gonna tell the boss?!*" A big guy in a suit too tight for his build stepped away from Jake.

"Da boss *said* that if he didn' have a Power, they were all ours, so we do what we do best," the woman said. She seemed to be in charge. "The lil' girl likes my scar, let's give her one."

It took me a second to realize she was talking about me, but by then it was too late. They had dragged me into the middle of the room, pulled up a table, and laid me down on it.

"Mike unlock 'er and put her hands under the table. Yeah like that. Jacob, lock 'er back up. Adam, hold 'er head down. Billy do ya have the puck?" The woman barked.

One man handed her a metal circle, it was the exact size of her scar. The woman wrapped her hand in a tight fist around the disk, and when she uncurled her fingers, the metal glowed red-hot. She put it on my left cheek and pressed. Burning, searing pain shot through my face, blinding me.

But this was where they made their mistake. The table and floor were metal: conductors. I shot my pain across the room in the form of lightning, trying hard to get those responsible and not my siblings. I screamed and I screamed, shooting electricity. I could feel my energy draining but I didn't care. Eventually I blacked out, but it didn't matter. I had killed our enemies.

CHAPTER 20

Grace was in shock, a normal reaction for someone who had just seen their younger sister *kill* six grown-ups. Grant was the first one to break the silence.

"Jake help me bar the door, Grace . . . hey Grace. Grace? Earth to Grace. GRACE SNAP OUT OF IT!" He snapped in her face until she blinked.

"What?" She shook herself to help get back to normal, and tried to sound casual.

"I was just going to ask you if you thought that it was a good idea to leave." *Finally* she thought, *he's accepting my superiority.* But Grant must have realized his mistake at the same time she did, because he quickly added in "Of course, I would just make the decision myself but I know how your ego gets in the way sometimes when I decide everything, and I just really don't think this is the right time for us to be fighting."

Normally, this would have sent Grace into a rampage, but she realized that at least the last part of his speech was right. They really needed to work together right now.

"Yeah, I'll unlock Jess and you guys bar the door then we'll make a plan." *That's my brilliant plan to make them think I had this under control? Pathetic. I don't even know how to unlock her cuffs!* But it was really the best she could think of right now.

Grace walked to the center of the room and slid under the table where Jess lay, her hair matted to her head as her unconscious body heaved, trying to pull in enough oxygen to facilitate the regeneration of power. Concentrating hard, Grace shot a tiny blob of water into the air above her finger, suspended like an eerie little blue-green ghost. Then, using something she had only seen more advanced students do, she made the water spin, faster and faster, until it formed a spinning disk with a razor-sharp edge.

As she pulled the handcuffs gently away from her sister's arms, she sawed cuts all the way around them from the metal. Carefully, she cut the metal, hoping that the water wouldn't break. Tiny water droplets flew in every direction, including into Jess' cuts. Her little sister moaned and pulled her wrists away, but Grace knew she had to keep going. Half way through, the disk was completely destroyed and she had to make another one. Panting with exhaustion, she sat back, hoping her Power would come back.

Just as she was forming the second disk, she heard her brothers whispering behind her. "Maybe we should wait for help." That was Jake's high, shaky voice, racked with worry. "We'll see, bud, we'll see. Everything is gonna be okay." Grant tried to soothe him, but Grace could hear the insecurity in his voice, too.

Grace knew they had to leave. But where to? All she was certain of was that nobody would ever find them here, wherever *here* was. But she couldn't worry about that now. She had to free her sister.

CHAPTER 21

Four cobweb covered kids army-crawled through the dusty air vent. You'd never know they were there unless you listened to the occasional "bang" as a misplaced foot hit the side of the metal pipe.

"Shhhhh," Scarlett whispered, "just because I cloaked you in Darkness doesn't mean they can't *hear* you."

Dani rolled her eyes. "Come on Scar, we're trying."

Scarlett shot a reproachful glare in her general direction. "You wouldn't even *be* on this mission if we hadn't snuck you past Hodd! I'm starting to think we should've left you behind!"

Anger bubbled in Dani's stomach, and she turned, ready for a fight, when Peter interrupted.

"Look there's a vent opening up head."

Peter wiped his arm across his sweaty forehead. The 80-degree air in the vent may have been keeping the rest of the building comfortable, but it was creating a sauna up in the vent.

"Come here!" Esmerelda whispered from ahead.

Everyone crawled over and look down into a round room. What Dani saw wasn't scary, just a little freaky. Grant and a little boy, who had to be Jake, were pushing a metal table in front of the door. Grace was sitting in the adjacent corner with Jess lying in front of her. Dani shook her head. What exactly was going on? Grace seemed to be doing the last thing that could possibly help Jess, no matter what had happened. A gentle stream of water was pouring from Grace's fingertips over Jess's face. "I'm going in, Peter help me move this grate." Esmeralda ordered in a whisper.

Slowly the metal was pulled away. The four kids crouched around the edges of the hole. Jake looked up, hearing the noise, but saw nothing and turned back to what he was doing.

Peter elbowed Scarlett in the side. "The darkness! They can't see us!"

Finally the vent was opened and Esmerelda slid herself into the room feet first. She landed gracefully, on her feet, with a thud.

Grace looked away from Jess, "Ezzy!"

She ran over to her friend, leaving a moving ball of water churning over Jess' face. Grace wrapped Esmeralda in a tight hug.

"Okay, no one hugs my girlfriend before me." Peter said loudly. With that he dropped in almost on top of the two girls hugging below.

"PETER!" Grace broke apart from Esmeralda and hit her boyfriend in a fervent hug followed by a kiss.

"Don't forget me," Scarlett said dropping into the space besides Esmeralda.

"You're not getting a kiss," Grace laughed, "But you can have a hug."

Wait, Dani told herself, *once they move.*

"Yo Scarlett," Grant pushed his little brother to the ground and walked to the center of the room. Even from above Dani could see the tint of pink in Scarlett's pale cheeks.

Eventually the small group gave Dani some landing space. She tried to land on her feet, but her side had a meeting with the floor it couldn't miss.

"What was that?" Grant said.

"Oh, right." Scarlett moved her hand down as if to close a window, "I cloaked Dani so she could come."

Dani could suddenly see herself. She could also see Scarlett sink halfway to the ground before Grant caught her.

"Nice, a cloak," Grant nodded in appreciation.

"What wrong with Jess?" Esmeralda asked.

"Loss of energy," Grace pointed around the room at the bodies of adults, "Killed them all, but after . . ." She stopped at a groan from Jess.

"Looks like she's coming to" Peter said.

Jess was indeed coming around. She rubbed her eyes, sat up, and ran her hands over her entire face, wiping the water off. She looked terrible, tried, beaten up, and just different in a way that Dani couldn't quite put her finger on. Then Jess took her hand off her face and Dani saw it. Jess had a pink circle indented just left of her mouth.

"What happened?"

CHAPTER 22

Grant steadied Scarlett. She shot him a smile that made butterflies erupt in his stomach, but he had more pressing matters to deal with. Jess had seen everyone's reactions to her face and was trying to get a good look at herself in the reflective metal of the wall.

He walked over, "Jess—" She ignored him, reaching up to run a finger over the pink circle on her cheek, wincing as she pulled her hand away.

"Grace, Jake, can you . . ." Grant jerked his head towards the crowd and pointed a finger at the opposite side of the room, his eyes resting on his little brother a second longer to try to get the message through.

He turned his attention back to Jess, who had slid down the wall to hide her face in her hands, again. Jake, who couldn't take a hint, sat down next to her and tried to snuggle, thinking it would make Jess fell better, but was pushed away.

Grant pulled the younger boy to the other side of the room, at which point the six year old threw a ground-shaking tantrum.

"Jake, me n' Jess need to talk *alone*," Grant put heavy emphases on the last word. "She needs her *older* brother right now."

"No, Jessie needs me. Me. Me! ME!" Jake's voice got shriller and shriller with each word, until he sounded like a distressed bird.

Grant could feel his temper rising. He jerkily turned his brother around and shoved him at the crowd in the center of the room.

Grant turned hurriedly. He knew that what he had done was wrong, but if he saw the judgmental stares of the others, especially Scarlett, he was afraid he'd totally lose it. Striding over to Jess he squatted down next to her.

"Jess? This . . . this scar changes nothing." Grant said gently.

"Nothing? NOTHING?! It changes everything. Look at me, Grant." Jess looked up, her eyes streaming and her voice cracking.

"I am looking. I'm looking at my little sister, Jessica Amy Clease."

"Are you not seeing this? Look."

She showed a fake smile, except it wasn't a smile exactly. The right corner of her lips came up, but the left didn't even twitch. It looked like she was smirking at him, but Grant could tell from her eyes what she was trying to do.

"What do you want me to say, Jess? That you're a different person? Because you're not."

"*This* is permanent. As in forever, I'm gonna have to remember *this* forever!" Jess' voice hit a desperate note. She put emphases on every *this* and gestured to the circle on her cheek. "People will stare, and point, and spread rumors and—"

"And you shouldn't care, you never did before." She started to say something, but Grant gently covered her mouth with his hand. "Jess, you're one of the strongest, most confident, self-assured people I know, and no scar, permanent or not, will change that."

Jess said nothing, but put her head on Grant's shoulder.

"Jessie? We need to get out of here." Grace said, bending over them.

Jess sighed, "Okay, let's go home."

CHAPTER 23

Grant stood, helping Jess up as he did, and dusted off his hands. Looking up the way his friends had come, but there was no hole at all. "Stupid magic buildings" he muttered under his breath.

But he knew he didn't have time to get upset. Making a quick choice he grabbed the table that blocked the door, and lugged it out of his way and opened the door. "Let's do this."

Scarlett shot Grant a quick glance, a look that lasted less than a quarter of a second, but it sent butterflies fluttering to every corner of Grant's stomach, again. He had had a crush on her for months. At first, he had pushed it away thinking it would ruin their friendship. However, crushes aren't meant to be smothered, and this one had bloomed. Now when she looked his way, his heart would dance.

Lost in his thoughts, Grant didn't notice a bit of movement in the intersecting hallway. Suddenly a wall of cement blocked off the hall behind the group.

A harsh voice came from nowhere. "You little kiddies wanna go home, huh? You think you can just walk out of here? Fools. It's going to be harder than that."

Saying the floor gave out wouldn't have been accurate. This was more like trap doors opened under the feet of the rescuers and captives. Suddenly the floor wasn't a floor at all but a long flat metal slide leading down into complete darkness.

Clang! Grant careened head first into a metal wall. His head ringing, he stood and looked around. He was at the end of a metal hallway sloping gently up under the artificial glow of thousands of buzzing fluorescent lightbulbs. Nobody else was there.

"Jess? Jake? Grace? SCARLET? HELLO? ANYONE?" But nobody answered. Behind him, the slide had entirely disappeared.

Well only one-way out. Grant sighed and took the slope at a jog.

After a few minutes, Grant found himself at a dead end. "Seriously!?" Grant turned and pounded his fist into the wall. It went right through. "What the . . ." Grant stepped through after his suddenly invisible arm.

Suddenly, he was in an unlit cavern. Not that the lack of light was a problem. Looking around, Grant saw that there were three entrances, marked only by slightly gray patches of rock along the otherwise smooth and unchanged walls. There was the way he had come, another on the same level on the other side of the room, and one in higher up along that same wall. As he watched orange light burst out of the higher one and a figure came flying out.

Instincts took over. Running forward, Grant caught the person. Dark Sight kicked in and he could see he was holding Scarlett. She was unconscious and there was a bloody cut over her temple.

Taking off his shirt, he pressed to cloth to his crush's head and shifted in to a sitting position.

Again he moved so as to hold the girl better, his left hand on her lower back, his right holding her head. On his knees now he bent low, face-to-face with Scarlett. He could smell her shampoo; feel her breath on his face. Then not daring to slow in case he chickened out, he kissed her gently on the lips. Floating, spinning, flying, Grant's brain melted. Then he felt movement that wasn't his own.

Scarlett was awake, and she smiled weakly.

CHAPTER 24

Running around alone in the pitch black isn't fantastic for the nerves, especially if you've just had a near death experience.

The metal walls, hallways, slopes, turns, curves, and intersections created a terrifying maze. There were no lights other than my weakened Power.

"Ha-ha, look at 'em run. Oh yeah, don't mess with Granlet!"

"We are NOT Granlet! It sounds like 'gran let' as in little granny. That's just not a good name."

Grant and Scarlett! I thought it was them, but I wasn't sure so I had to be careful. Sneaking towards the corner I heard voices nearby, so I pressed my stomach against the wall and waited. I had to see if my brother would come out. If not, I'd slip out of the corridor to hide.

"Jessie?" I spun around to see Jake.

I put a finger to my lips and pressed my back against the wall. Jake followed my lead.

Two figures rounded the corner I was watching. "Jess? Jake?"

"Grant?"

"Uh-huh." Yup, definitely my brother.

Scarlett came up behind him, and we set out as a group. Five minutes later, we heard footsteps. Hiding in an adjoining hallway, we watched as two people quietly walked past.

Out of the blue, Grant leaped out of our hiding place. "Grace!"

In the tiny bit of light, I saw one of the figures turn and punch Grant in the head.

"OW! D*mn it, Grace! It's me."

"Grant?" Grace still held her fists up.

"Yes! It's me, duh. Are you blind or something?" Grant stood up from the floor where he had fallen when Grace punched him.

"Sorry, I can't see in the dark."

"Dark? Peter's light is makin' this whole place shine like a beacon. You guys are giving us all away!"

"Like I said, not all of us can see in the dark Grant!" Grace said, exasperated.

Grace ran forward and hugged our little brother. She kissed his head. He started to cry and she hoisted him onto her knee and bounced him up and down, hushing him softly.

"Let's go this way." Scarlett said pointing down the hall we were standing at the entrance of.

As we walked, Grant talked. His bad mood seemed to melt away as soon as we got moving. He was telling jokes, stories, and riddles.

"Hey Peter, riddle me this. I am to Scarlett as you are to Grace."

"Seriously? You two? Congrats!"

I saw Grace and Scarlett hang back to gossip. I wasn't interested, so I stuck by Jake to make sure nothing happened.

Suddenly screams broke out above our heads. I felt a hand on my shoulder. Peter.

"Need your Power." He left his one hand on my shoulder, with the other he shot a huge bolt of lightning at the ceiling.

Now I could see Dani and Ezmerelda. Ezzy seemed to be unconscious, but Dani was wide-awake and screaming. Suddenly I saw that on her way down, Dani would go straight through the lightning. It would probably kill her.

CHAPTER 25

"Dani!" I said to Peter, barely able to choke out the name, but he understood me.

"Go."

I climbed the lightning, like I did ropes in gym. I forced my Power into my movements and shot up like a bullet. The electricity felt solid under my hands and feet.

I clambered up the bolt, to the spot where Dani would go through the lightning. She came sailing towards me. I leaned out to her at an angle and snatched her wrist. Her momentum and my weight brought us swinging around the electricity. Now Dani was dangling out in the open about four feet away from the lightning.

"Catch Ezzy," I called down as Dani and I slid down the bolt.

Ezmerelda tumbled at a quickening pace. Barely five feet above the heads of those trying to snatch her out of the air, she hit the wall with a sickening thud. Then she dropped to the ground.

Grace frantically started checking for broken bones by running her hands over her friend's body and seeing where she winced the worst. "Legs are fine. Her left arm is broken. Sh*t, a couple of her ribs are messed up, we shouldn't move her."

"Grace, we may not have a choice," Peter said looking down the corridor.

There were three hulking figures standing there. One took a step forward and we ran for it. Scarlett and Grant carried Ezmerelda. Peter sucked in the lightning bolt. Grace scooped up Jake. I was still holding Dani's wrist and pulled her along.

We ran, taking turns at random, following no particular formula, strategy, or pattern. A right, a left, maybe that curve, now run a bit. Time to use Powers to scale that wall to that opening and head straight.

Rounding the corner, we were met by several adults. Peter stepped forward in the formal Electricity fighting stance.

The leader who was the biggest chuckled, "Whoa, there kid. Hodd sent us. Here, he told me to give this to you." He handed Peter a handwritten note from Hodd, which my sister's boyfriend reluctantly took and read.

"They're legit." Peter was relieved for obvious reasons. "Let's get out of here."

SHOUT OUTS

There were a lot of people who helped with this book.

Thanks especially to Theresa Christensen for putting in a lot of time editing the first version. I also had a lot of friends, teachers, and relatives involved with this. There are too many to list, but if you ever saw this creation of mine, or ever talked about characters with me, thank you. You know who you are.